"Don't let the cheek[y] ... not really an erotic wo[rk] ... [rath]er that seeks t... tight an ... [amon]g the moc... [pa]t its clever ingén[ue] ... [mean]ing quite else. It will chi[ll] ... [readers as the]y turn the pages, eager for the ne[xt] ... [eroti]c encounter, when you aren't otherwise c[hortling] ... [wild]e at the humor and wit. A surprising, fun short sho[cker fe]aturing the Aboriginal Yara-ma-yha-who -- a creature I bet you've never heard of before, but will never forget after reading this story!"

— Michael Arnzen, Bram Stoker Award-winning author of Licker and 100 Jolts

"With genderqueer horror fiction clawing its way to center stage, Rowland's tale is a transgressive mindfuck that will leave you irreparably unnerved"

— L. Stephenson, author of The Goners

"Rebecca Rowland has a narrative mastery that makes you feel as if a good friend is pulling you in close to tell you some special secret that only you will understand, but the deeper you find yourself in Shagging the Boss, the more you may begin to think, 'this person is not my friend,' but it will be too late: you're cornered and you have to hear the whole bloody thing. You'll be left shook and unsure how you feel about what you just heard. But what you will do is stick close to that friend for the rest of the night because she's got all the best stories and you want to hear more!"

— Tim Murr, Stranger With Friction

SHAGGING THE BOSS

Copyright © 2022 by Rebecca Rowland
Cover & Layout by Ira Rat

A previous version of *Shagging The Boss* appeared in serial form in Midnight Tales (2021).

This is a work of fiction. Names, characters, businesses, places, events, locales, and incidents are either the products of the author's imagination or used in a fictitious manner. Any resemblance to actual persons, living or dead, or actual events is purely coincidental

This book may not be reproduced in whole or in part, except for the inclusion of brief quotations in a review, without permission in writing from the author or publisher. No part of this publication may be reproduced, stored in or introduced into retrieval system, or transmitted, in any form, or by any means (electronic, mechanical, photocopying, recording, or otherwise), without prior permission of the publisher.

Requests for permission should be directed to filthylootpress@gmail.com

FIRST EDITION, 2022

SHAGGING THE BOSS

REBECCA ROWLAND

Filthy Loot

filthyloot.com

Shag:

1) To have sexual intercourse

2) A form of rough pipe tobacco

3) A sea bird, A small cormorant

4) A thick pile on a carpet

-Urban Dictionary

"It's not enough to be smart, or bloody gorgeous, or dirty rich. You need to be at least two simultaneously. All three if you're over thirty."

That's what my employer, Daniel, told me one evening while we were sitting in a bone dry hot tub, him smoking a bowlful of Vanilla Cavendish, both of us still wearing our clothes from the dinner party. I loved the way he said the words *dirty* and *thirty*, his Brisbane accent slicing the ends of the *r*'s and holding them up in the air between two fingers. He frowned as if disagreeing with an unseen quarreler, then looked at me. "How old are you again?" he asked.

"Twenty-three," I said, stretching my arms behind my head in an exaggerated yawn.

"Too old to shag," he said, a funny, half-smile on his face.

"Sorry?" I asked.

"We used to visit my cousins in Canada every Christmas," Daniel said. "If they had a snow, they'd drag us out to the Main Street, sneak over to a car stopped at a traffic light and grab hold of the bumper. When the car began to move, they'd be pulled along with it, like Santa on his sleigh." He relit the end of his pipe and inhaled deeply. "'Called it shagging," he added, his breath held tight within his lungs and his voice halted and miserly. He tucked his fingers in between the third and fourth buttons of his dress shirt and rested them there, his hand hiding its top like an ostrich. Daniel's shoulders were broad, Paul Bunyan broad, but his belly was swollen and round like a woman a short season away from giving birth.

"I could do that," I said, smiling with my lips pursed tight.

Daniel blew a thick cloud of smoke at me and I steeled myself to keep from coughing uncontrollably. "I'll bet you could, my ingénue." He removed his hand from his shirt, grabbed my arm, and unbuttoned the cuff of my shirt, then pushed it roughly past my elbow. Predatorily, he ran a finger along the center.

I jerked my arm away and pushed the sleeve down. "Seems like it would be fun," I added.

Daniel smiled, but it was not the kind for an expression of happiness or even bemusement. His eyes glazed over into round black marbles before his hand snatched my arm again and wrenched it painfully toward his open mouth, his thick red tongue running back and forth along his teeth, trying to dislodge them. I closed my eyes and felt his hot breath just below the crook of my elbow, a splotch of dripped saliva wetting the fabric there.

Daniel taught me everything I know about publishing.

My parents named me after a city they fell in love with the year after they graduated college, the nine months they spent backpacking around the United States instead of submitting the first payments on their student loans. "We should have named you *Navient* instead," my mother remarked my senior year of high school as I completed my financial aid application. "Christ, we've had a longer relationship with them than just about anyone."

I have two siblings, one older and the other younger. Fortunately for me, each of us has one of those gender-neutral city names, the kind that makes teachers bend their voices into question marks when they read it for roll call on the first day of school. My parents were those "progressive" Gen-X-ers who painted their children's bedrooms in green and yellow hues and filled the toy box with equal shares of dolls and dump trucks. I often joked that with as many times as they folded their arms into pretzels patting their own backs about it, they should have bought stock in Ben Gay. My mom always rolled her eyes when I said this. My dad simply ignored my criticism and tuned out my snark by turning up Pearl Jam or Soundgarden or whatever unwashed guitar-y goth music was playing in our house at the time.

He died of a massive heart attack on their way to see me collect my diploma for a Master's degree in English. My mother told me it happened during the first or second hour of the flight.

Fortunately, none of us are named Albany, Toledo, or Chicago.

When I had boarded the same airline two years previous, I thought I would never see the Boston suburb of my childhood again, not unless it was Thanksgiving or maybe a wedding or funeral. Mom's three children lived scattered around the country, but she refused to sell the three-floor Victorian in West Medford after Dad's sudden departure, and while I hated being a stereotype, I found myself lugging my belongings back into my parents' cavernous home after graduate school, leaving most of my networked Northern California connections 3085 miles away. As I dragged my steamer trunk of books up the wooden stairs and onto the broad front porch, I told myself, it was just temporary, a change of scenery required only until my flummoxed parent was back on her feet, but one month after I arrived, Mom stopped going to work. She stopped going to her beloved book club. She stopped going to the supermarket. A month after that, she stopped going to the washing machine in the basement. Or to the shower in the bathroom of the top-floor master suite.

"My love?" she said, her voice business-like on the phone. "The house is yours. I'm just going to Bertha Mason it for a few years, if you don't mind."

I pulled the cell from my ear and stared at the screen, listening for her voice's echo from two floors above. She hung up, ordered a microwave, coffeemaker, and a rudimentary set of dishes and cups from Amazon, and never came downstairs again, at least not while I was home. I set up shop in the small back den off the kitchen, the two of us making an unspoken agreement to leave the second floor vacant, my childhood home now a sandwich of empty calories.

Each morning, I called my mother to ask how she was doing. "I'm getting on" is all she would say. That, and "Have you uncovered any of my missing earrings?" She was referring to the shag carpet in the stuffy front living room, its strands measuring nearly two inches in length so that when I walked across it, my feet sunk down to be smothered in its quicksand of blue yarn tentacles. Over the years, paperclips, Lego bricks, and even a Matchbox car or two had disappeared within its depths, my mother's earrings (and occasionally, a delicate necklace or two) fellow victims, the items only resurfacing when Mom rented an industrial carpet cleaner.

"Not yet," I always replied, though much of that was from lack of trying. The time I spent in the front living room was limited, at best. At the time of the Riley Book Fair, nothing had been unearthed from the plush piles of carpet.

Not yet.

Once a staple of New York City's Javits Center, the Riley Book Fair had moved to Boston the year I left for California. It was one of the largest and longest running expositions for publishing in America, its booths brimming with big-name authors, promotion opportunists, and representatives from presses big and small. Writing ingénues and literature fanatics flocked to its floor in droves, entry tickets sometimes selling out before noon on each of the fair's four days.

I caught the commuter rail to North Station at seven A.M., then stood grasping the handrails near the end of a green-line subway car as tightly packed students and weary business people avoided eye contact with one another around me. I watched a small child, perhaps eight years old, attempt to balance himself in the elbow between two cars, twisting and turning his torso to compensate for the train's movement. I used to do the same, even as a teenager, imagining that I was surfing an angry ocean.

As shop owners bent to unlock the closed cages of the sleepy stores and eateries along the tiled passageway through Prudential Center, the resolute metronome of my wing-tipped shoes changed from sharp clicks to muted pats when I entered the double doors to the carpeted Hynes Convention Center. The place always smelled like an airplane during an early morning boarding: sterile, empty, and secure. Attendees began to file in behind me, presenters with name badges encased in plastic and hung around necks with string. A man in a Sox cap pushed an onerous food cart through the swelling crowd and disappeared into one of the side halls. I stepped into one of the lines at registration and busied myself by unzipping my shoulder bag to check again for my resume.

"Quite a show, isn't it?" A tall man with salt and pepper hair had sidled up beside me without my noticing. He rested one hand in his suit pants pocket; the other clutched a Dunkin Donuts Styrofoam cup, and he raised it to his mouth, staring straight ahead.

"Pardon?" I said, now uncertain if he had been speaking to me.

The man pulled the cup away and swallowed, then glanced slowly my way. "This," he said, motioning with the coffee. "This circus. What a bloody nightmare." His voice was gruff, a smoker's voice, and had a pronounced Australian lilt to it. He glanced down at his wrist. He wore not an Apple Watch or a traditional Timex but a beautiful cerulean blue Rolex—a vintage model, I later learned—with a gleaming gold band.

I smiled politely and glanced at the front of the line to assess my wait.

"Writer?" he asked. "Or are you a reader?" He removed the other hand from his pocket and rested it on his chest. Under his grayish-brown suit jacket, he wore a white dress shirt unbuttoned at the top. Thin blue pinstripes iced his torso, one that ballooned into a portly stomach.

"I'm a little of both, I suppose," I said. "I'm here to see the area publishers, inquire if there are any entry-level opportunities." I nervously zipped up my shoulder bag as the line inched forward.

The man raised an eyebrow, but I could see a slight grin tipping the edges of his mouth. "Business degree, then? Marketing, yeah?"

"English literature."

"A bachelor's in English," he said solemnly. "Not much of a career path there."

"Master's," I corrected.

He laughed. "Even worse." He glanced down at my chest, and then my waist.

I smirked slightly, then turned back toward the front of the line, feeling his greasy eyes slide again from my ear to my thigh and then his large hand on my shoulder.

"What's your name?" he asked.

I told him.

"Is that a girl's or a boy's name?" he said, glancing down questioningly at my torso again.

I pulled at the front of my suit jacket, trying to shake off his grasp. "It's an adult's," I said. I kept my eyes fixed on his face. He was a handsome man, that was for certain. His hair hinted at age, but his pinkish skin was absent of wrinkles, and even as he scrunched his eyes and mouth in exaggerated expression, the muscles below the surface moved smoothly, without a hint of Botox or other cosmetic procedure remnants. Cloaked behind the full lips of his wide mouth were teeth I suspected were dentures: square white chiclets that seem horribly misplaced tucked beneath the satin curtain of flesh.

He moved his hand to my elbow and pulled gently. "Come on, then," he said, and tilted his head toward a nearby door on one of the partitions.

I frowned.

"I'm giving you a way in," he said. "Follow me." He began to walk toward the door, gliding effortlessly through the bustling crowd without bothering to look back. I glanced quickly at the stagnant line of attendees waiting to be processed ahead of me, then stepped out of line and followed.

On the other side of the partition was a much larger ballroom, its floor a robust burgundy carpet covered with a dizzying pattern of gold and navy zig-zagging this way and that. Wide, makeshift offices stood in rows separated by curtained half-walls. Vendors spread their brightly-colored wares at end-caps while the more refined businesses—publishing firms, likely—occupied hushed cubicles along the temporary corridors. I had to double my steps to keep pace with my guide, who maintained his stride without hesitating to glance at any of the displays. He finally stopped in front of an exceptionally large booth draped in grayish-brown tapestry the same color as his suit.

"Luke," he said, handing his Styrofoam cup to a pale, angular-faced man behind the front table. "Hand me one of the lanyards, would you?"

Luke accepted the cup without comment and tossed it deftly into the trash bin a few feet away, then leaned down to rifle through a small container hidden out of immediate sight. He returned to standing clutching a beige-colored badge strung along a thick black cord. *Xanadu Publishing* was typed neatly along the top margin. Instead of handing the pass to me, Luke stared at me blankly, so I tilted my head forward, and he lassoed my neck with it. I could smell his cologne: something expensive and full of sandalwood.

"Xanadu, huh?" I said, leaning back and fingering

the smooth lamination. "Are you a *Citizen Kane* fan, Mr..." I faltered for his name, embarrassed to be unable to recall if he had mentioned it earlier.

The man rested his hand on his chest again and grinned. "I don't fancy Hearst, if that's what you're asking, though I can understand the obvious comparison." He raised one of his eyebrows, then reached out a hand toward me. "You may call me Daniel."

I accepted his hand and squeezed it confidently. His palm dwarfed mine, all five of my fingers disappearing under a mound of smooth, cold skin. I noticed Daniel's eyes narrow, a sheet of wet excitement shimmering in his irises, and I glanced around the booth's interior to cover the discomfort simmering in my stomach. "You're a celebrity publisher?" I asked, noticing the innumerable prints of book covers pasted tastefully along the makeshift walls. Nearly all of them featured actors or politicians I recognized.

Daniel released his grip and let his arm hang by his side. "I suppose you could say that. We are primarily a memoir press, with a selection of coffee-table pop culture titles sprinkled here and there." He nodded at his assistant. "Luke here is in charge of promotion. Lisa," he motioned to a woman sitting at a small table in the back corner of the booth. She was typing on a silver-colored laptop and had not acknowledged our presence even though she must have noticed our arrival. "Is the only full-time editor on staff. Most presses employ free-lancers to do their grunt work, but I like to keep my staff in a closed circle. They answer their own phones and email, though they have had some difficulty keeping up with the slush as of late."

I tried to keep my visual assessment of the two employees to a minimum, but it was difficult to take my eyes from them. Both were relatively young—in their mid-thirties, at most—and had chiseled, poreless faces nearly completely void of color save for a faint pinkish hue. Though this was the only physical attribute they had in common, there was something eerily familial about them. "So, you're looking for entry-level help?" I asked, finally returning my eyes to Daniel. I felt along my shoulder bag for the zipper so I that could remove my resume, but Daniel reached out and touched my upper arm to stop me.

"I don't need to see your credentials," he said. "I like to pride myself on being an exceptional judge of character. Besides, no one would manufacture having spent good money on such a rubbish degree." He laughed, and I smiled to humor him. "Give Luke your contact information, and he'll send you the requisite hiring forms. Return them this week, and you can start next Monday. I'll take you on as a trial basis for two months—with pay, of course—then we'll see about making something permanent if we're both satisfied with the relationship."

I willed my face not to frown in disbelief. "You don't want to interview me first?" I asked. Luke held out an iPad to me, the screen already displaying a three-line form for my name, cell, and email. I quickly typed my information, and Luke pulled back the tablet and held it vertically a foot away from my face. Before I could react, he clicked the Home button and a camera shutter sounded.

Daniel checked his watch again. "Tell you what. I haven't had a proper breakfast. Why don't you join me?"

I glanced at the booth again. Lisa was still typing,

her eyes glued to the screen. Luke stood perfectly still, coolly surveying the crowd growing behind me, his hands draped casually in his suit pockets like a department store mannequin. The iPad was nowhere to be seen. I fingered the badge again. After meeting with Daniel, I could return to the convention at my leisure; the pass would allow me to come and go all week as I pleased.

"Sure," I agreed. I nodded my goodbye at Luke, but he did not look at me, and Daniel and I retraced our steps back through the hidden exit in the partition and through the main lobby. The lines were now twice as long at the check-in, but we walked quickly past them and through the impossibly long entryway of the Hynes. Daniel held one of the double doors open for me, then crooked his head to the right once we were in the main passageway. All of the Prudential attractions were open for business, and groups of chatty tourists were already congregated, their metallic-sounding voices echoing in the capacious space. We walked together in silence for a few minutes until the red carpeted entranceway to the Sheraton Hotel extension came into view.

I stopped. "Where are we having breakfast, exactly?"

Daniel took two more steps before stopped as well. "You don't expect to have a civilized conversation at Au Bon Pain, do you?" He glanced back down the corridor from where we'd come and rolled his eyes. "Let's go. There's a bar in the lobby that I'm certain makes Bloody Marys." He continued to walk toward the passageway doors, never checking to see if I was following. I eventually did.

There was indeed a bar on the ground floor, but when we reached the lobby, it was clear that most of the tables were spoken for and we'd likely have to scream over the noise to be heard by one another. However, Daniel walked immediately to a nearby hotel employee and whispered a lengthy commentary into his ear. Right away, the bellhop made his way to the front desk and conferred with the concierge, who nodded in our direction.

"Come," Daniel said to me and walked toward the bank of elevators around the corner. "They'll meet us upstairs." He waived a key card in front of the number pad, lighting up one of the buttons, and the doors closed behind us. "I ordered a continental spread," he said. "You're not on one of those vapid carbohydrate-free diets, are you? We all need a bit of sugar in our lives from time to time."

When the doors opened again, Daniel walked sharply to the left, to one of only a handful of doors on the exclusive floor. I stepped out of the elevator but hesitated. "I'm not in the habit of becoming someone's trigger warning." I swallowed hard. "I don't mean to be crass, Daniel. I want a job, but even this English degree-carrying ingénue doesn't wish to fuck their way into one."

"Christ," he said. "I don't even watch Fox News, much less wish to be the CEO." When I said nothing in return, he added, "Roger Ailes? No? Nothing?" He inserted his keycard into the door lock and I heard its distinct click. "I promise you. There will be no sexual favoring of any kind," He walked inside and out of view just as the elevator across from me dinged. The door slid sideways and the bellhop from the lobby pushed out a rolling tray with an assortment of covered dishes and two silver carafes.

Even today, I think back to that morning, that afternoon, and the months that followed, and I find my actions difficult to explain. I could blame my decision to join Daniel in his grandiose room on naïveté, on reckless ennui, or on sheer desperation to secure a foot on a career ladder, but I know deep inside, I joined him simply out of curiosity. Without another word, I followed behind the room service delivery and into the palatial suite.

The main room was exceptionally large, one wall completely covered with windows overlooking the Back Bay. Thick beams of full sun bathed the room in warm light. The hotel employee quickly transferred the platters to a small dinette set near the door then stood silent, his expression frozen in an odd grin until Daniel removed a fan of bills from his pocket and placed it into his hand, not bothering to check the amount. The bellhop quickly thanked him and exited without even glancing my way, the door closing behind him with a funereal shush.

I shifted my weight from one foot to another, waiting to be asked to sit down. Instead, Daniel collapsed backwards into a plush-looking sofa with an audible groan. "I'm already exhausted," he confessed. "I really shouldn't venture out before having breakfast." He stretched his arms above his head and let them fall lazily along the top of the couch. Only then did he acknowledge my presence, appearing to have forgotten that I accompanied him. "Come, my ingénue," he said, jerking his head sideways in invitation. "Come and sit for a spell."

I walked slowly toward him, pausing at the table of breakfast platters, the silver domed lids still capped in place. "Would you like me to bring you something?" I heard my own stomach growl as the buttery scent of warm croissants leaked out from one of the dishes.

"In a moment, in a moment," he protested. "Come, sit." He patted the cushion immediately to his left.

I obliged him, sitting a polite distance away but closer than I was truly comfortable with. The sofa's fabric was soft, and I ran my right hand absentmindedly along the small swatch of material between us.

As if to stop my movement, Daniel placed his hand gently on my wrist. "May I?" he asked, his eyes staring blankly into mine.

"May you what?" I asked, suddenly nervous.

He did not reply, but unclasped the buttons at my wrist and pushed my shirt and jacket upward, the fabric bunching in an awkward clump in the crook of my elbow, exposing my pale skin, a tangle of purplish blue veins lurking not far below. Before I could protest, Daniel pulled my arm closer to his face and bent down, nearly resting his nose on my skin. He closed his eyes, tilted my arm slightly, and breathed in deeply, smelling the inside of my wrist. I tried to jerk my hand away, but he held it surprisingly tight.

My eyes darted around the suite, then back to Daniel, whose eyes were only narrow slits, gradually opening again. "What are you—"

It was the sight of his eyes, finally open once more, that caused me to stop and my stomach to drop sickeningly into the bowels of my abdomen. His white sclera had disappeared, as had any trace of iris; in their place were wet, black marbles. Faster than I could react, Daniel's other hand snapped forward and latched onto my naked forearm, all ten of his fingers pressing hard into my flesh. I watched in confused horror as his fingertips tore ten round incisions into my body, breaking the skin, each digit disappearing up to the first knuckle. I yelped even though there was no pain, only a deep, pulsing heat pushing down into my radius and shooting upward toward my shoulder.

Daniel, his dead black eyes appearing to look at me, licked his lips. "Shhhhh…" he whispered, almost parental. "It will go faster if you don't try to wriggle away," he explained.

Despite his warning, I tried to retract my arm, but the fight was pointless. Daniel held me cemented in place. Encircling each of his inserted fingers were pools of bright red blood. The pools swelled, then slithered in thin rivers around my arm and onto my pants leg. When Daniel saw this, his face twisted into a ghoulish grimace. He pressed his lips tightly together and began to rotate his jaw in a small circle. When he opened them again, it was to spit his full set of teeth onto the coffee table. He grinned, exposing only red, raw gums, and a thick stream of saliva leaked out onto his chin.

It was then that the sun must have slid behind a

thick, dark cloud, because the room dimmed, and for a long moment, it was hard to see. I felt an overwhelming sense of relaxation, like sliding into a warm bath, and as Daniel lifted my hand toward his open, glistening mouth in the muted light, I felt myself relax backwards. My hand was about to be a rabbit in a magic trick, I thought drowsily.

And with that, I disappeared completely into the gaping maw of his deep, dark hat.

The suite was dim again when I awoke, but a different kind of darkness; the sky framed within the wall of windows was deep blue as the last vestiges of daylight waved back to the Eastern horizon. I lay slumped sideways on the sofa, my cheek plastered against its soft velour, and my first instinct was to right myself and check that my clothes were intact. I sat up straight and looked down at my shirt. It was buttoned as it had been previously; my jacket remained firmly planted on my body; even my shoes were still tied. Nothing seemed amiss. Daniel was sitting in a wing-back chair a few yards away, reading a well-worn paperback book, something by Richard Laymon. I could barely make out the cover from my vantage point and wondered how he was able to read without any source of artificial light. He held a pipe in his mouth and the room smelled faintly of burnt wood chips and cake.

I shook my head softly. "What…what happened?" I asked, partly out of embarrassment and partly out of vague distrust. I'd never passed out before, not even in college, and certainly never in a stranger's presence. My head ached, and all of the muscles in my upper body were sore, the way I often felt after the first day of ski season or when I pushed myself too hard at the gym. I lifted my right hand to rub my temple and jumped up immediately, startled and alarmed. "What—" I held my hand out to Daniel. "What happened to my hand?!"

The tips of each of my fingers were missing, each digit cauterized neatly an inch below the nail. Even my thumb was only a stump. There wasn't a smudge of blood anywhere. The droplets that had traveled down to my pants leg earlier were miraculously absent.

Daniel reached over to the table beside him

and turned on the lamp. He was still wearing the taupe-colored suit, his blue pinstriped shirt still crisp and neatly tucked into his pants. "Don't worry. They'll grow back; give it a day or two," he said casually. He smiled. His teeth had returned to his mouth and his eyes looked normal if not more rested than they had been that morning.

I brought my hand closer to my face to inspect it. The look of my fingers reminded me of the slight of hand my father used to do when my siblings and I were children. He'd tuck one thumb behind his index finger and the other he'd fold into his fist. When he brought the two hands together, it looked as though he were holding his right thumb with his left hand, but as he drew them apart, the thumb appeared to separate. I shook my hand as if the missing tips were somehow folded secretly inside. "Where did my fingers go? What happened?"

Daniel removed his pipe, closed his book, and placed both gingerly on the end table. "Please. Sit down. Or better yet, grab something to eat. The pastries are still in the tray. I didn't have the heart to throw them away." He stood up and walked in the opposite direction of me, toward a small refrigerator against the wall. "Would you like something to drink? Scotch? Vodka?"

"Water," I said without thinking. My mind vacillated between my body modification and the deep-seated thirst that suddenly plagued me. When Daniel handed me a cold plastic bottle, I accepted it with my left hand, checking for any missing digits. It appeared unchanged.

Daniel returned to his chair holding a matching bottle. He twisted off the cap and tilted his head back, then guzzled all of the water in the container without stopping for a breath. When the bottle was empty he tossed it softly on the ground nearby. Only then did I see the half dozen other empty water bottles already there. "Please," he repeated. "Sit. I will explain."

I hesitated, then sat back down on the couch, tucking my abbreviated hand under my thigh so that I didn't have to look at it. On the ledge of the window behind the wall of glass, a solitary bird pecked at an unseen morsel.

"Have you ever heard of *el Cuco*? *O papão*? The

Sack Man?" Daniel asked, resting his forearms on his knees and folding his hands together. I shook my head. "Every culture has its boogeyman," he continued, "the mysterious creature parents warn their children of in order to terrify them into behaving. The Japanese *Namahage* is an ogre who rounds up insolent youngsters to eat them for dinner. In Haiti, the *Mètminwi* will snatch them up if they are caught wandering around after curfew. In Belize, *Tata Duende* does the job. In Nepal, *Gurumapa* makes a feast of wayward tots, and in Algeria, the *H'awouahoua* wears clothing comprised of the shorn garments of the children he has consumed."

I frowned. "My parents would just threaten to call Santa or the Easter Bunny to cancel presents," I said.

Daniel laughed. "Americans," he said, and shook his head.

I finished the rest of the water in my bottle and tossed the container into Daniel's growing pile. Daniel stood up and nodded toward me. "You'd like another?" he asked. I nodded, and he walked back to the refrigerator. As he leaned down, he said, "There is an Aboriginal tale of the *Yara Ma Yha Who*, a creature who hides in the trees until visitors walk by." He walked back to me, carrying two bottles, the condensation covering them shimmering in the lamplight. I accepted one and instead of returning to his chair, he sat next to me on the couch, the same place he had earlier that day. "According to the story, as soon as people cross into *Yara Ma Yha Who*'s territory, he leaps onto their backs, sticks his long tentacles into their bodies, and sucks out nearly all of their blood. Then, the *Yara* swallows his victim—completely whole, like a pill." He stopped to take a long drink of his water, but I held my bottle upright on the cushion next to me, waiting.

He removed the bottle from his mouth, swallowed heartily, then looked at it. "Ah, that's nice," he said, momentarily distracted.

"So, boogeymen," I said. "I understand. What about them?"

Daniel leaned forward and placed his half empty bottle on the coffee table in front of my legs. "These stories, they don't come out of nowhere. All of them are based—and *based* is truly the correct choice of word here—at their core, on real monsters."

"I see," I said, raising my eyebrow. "You're saying that this *Yara Ma-you*—"

"*Yara Ma Yha Who*," Daniel corrected.

"…This *Yara Ma Yha Who* is a real thing?" I asked. "That an Australian boogeyman is creeping about the continent, draining passers-by of their blood and eating them?"

Daniel reached down and wrapped his meaty hand around my right forearm, then pulled my hidden hand out from under my thigh. "You tell me."

I pulled my hand away; this time, successfully. "I don't—" I began, confused.

Daniel's eyes bore into mine. "*I am a Yara Ma Yha Who*," he said. He smiled, showing me the white chiclet teeth again.

I stood up and backed away two steps, holding my affected hand to my stomach. "Jesus…" I glanced at the door, calculating my chances at escape.

Daniel stood as well but did not approach me. He held his hands open in front of his chest as if to show he were unarmed. "You misunderstand me. This isn't my plea for a second helping. You were satisfying in a pinch, but, my English degree ingénue, you're void of any real nutrients, sustenance. I have taken you on as a trainee, an apprentice, if you will, but you will never be who Luke or Lisa are, never be a true player in this business, unless you fill yourself with experience and *then* let me consume you."

"Consume me?" I echoed. "Like you consumed my fingertips."

"I told you," Daniel said calmly. "They will grow back in a few days. Parts always do. The celebrities prefer that I take their unsightly bits, the love handles or the twinkling of crow's feet at their temples. You see, when the parts grow back, they are good as new— *better* than new: young, energetic, vivacious. 'Saves them a trip to the plastic surgeon. I like to think of it as a true symbiotic relationship, mutually beneficial." He turned to look at the side table, then picked up a small remote and pressed a button. The overhead lights turned on, bathing the room in a warm glow. "Just wait and see. It's partly why I swallowed your fingers: you'll be reading through and typing responses for our slush pile. I want you at your best, and I couldn't very well eat your eyes, now could I?" He returned the device to the table and rested his hands in his pants pockets. "And of course, I was hungry as well." As if remembering something suddenly, he lifted his arm to check his watch. "Speaking of which, you must be famished. Shall we make dinner plans?"

I ignored his question. "If I let you consume me, you will teach me how to be successful in publishing? *Make* me a success?"

Daniel laughed again. "Oh, my dear ingénue," he said. "In order for you to be that, I must completely devour you: swallow you whole. And then, I must regurgitate you."

"Throw me up?" I clarified.

"Yes, if you want to be crass about it," Daniel said. "Each time I do so, you will retain a small bit of me, and as I ingest and regorge you, over and over, you will slowly become—"

"I will slowly become…like you," I said softly.

Daniel smirked. "No one will ever be like me. But yes, after enough time, you will become *Yara Ma Yha*

Who as well." He walked slowly toward the door and turned to face me, tucking his fingers in between the buttons of his dress shirt. "Lesson number one: don't get attached to anyone. Being a cannibal is the only way to truly succeed in this business." He placed one hand on the door handle, then thought a moment, and smiled to himself. "The problem is, once you take a bite, it will never be enough."

"What was that about being bloody gorgeous and filthy rich?"

The voice startled me and must have taken Daniel by surprise as well, though his only reaction was to blink a few times, his eyes transforming back to a human's as he relaxed again into the back of the hot tub and turned slightly to look at the visitor. "And smart," he clarified. "I was telling my young assistant here that one must be at least two in order to survive in this world."

Our dinner party host, the fashion designer, placed one hand on his hip and walked like a runway model toward us, hips swaying, but I could see an inkling of physical pain the motion was causing leak out from behind his flat countenance. When he finally stopped in front of us, he removed his hand and rubbed the triangle of smooth skin just below his bottom lip. "All three if you're over thirty," he added, meeting my eyes for the first time. "You stole that line from *me*, Daniel."

I pushed my shirt sleeve back down to my wrist and hastily rebuttoned the cuff. When I looked back up, the designer was still staring at me, a look of bemused interest fixed in his eyes. "And look what you've been hiding away," he said. "And here I thought Luke hoarded all of the cheekbones at Xanadu." He reached out with the same hand that had been stroking his chin and ran his fingertips lightly along the side of my face. I stared back in cool disinterest, not wanting to encourage him but not wishing to offend a client either. He removed his hand at my lack of reaction.

Daniel relit his pipe and a billow of sweet white smoke enveloped us momentarily. "It was a lovely party, Jayce. We just wanted a bit of air." He blew another puff of vanilla toward our host.

The designer briefly waved at the space in front of

his face and turned to me again. "Your employer is a collector. You know that, don't you?"

"A collector?" I echoed. It had been difficult not to stare at the host throughout dinner. I recognized Jayce immediately from his appearance on a drag queen competition series years earlier; my college dorm mates had been diehard fans and had monopolized the common room's television with the show every Friday evening. Jayce had made it to the top four, eliminated only after a seductive lip sync of She Wants Revenge's "Tear You Apart." As a woman, Jayce had been gorgeous with an angular face and subtly padded curves; as a man, he was even more breath-taking, his dark skin flawlessly satin and the muscles of his broad shoulders visibly tight under a custom-tailored shirt.

"Oh yes," Jayce said. "Have you read the book by John Fowles?"

I shook my head. "No, I'm not aware—"

Jayce leaned on the side of the tub, resting but not quite sitting on its edge. He crossed one foot over the other knee and reached down, rubbing the ankle a bit. "A great many serial killers have claimed inspiration from it. Leonard Lake and his sidekick there…Charles Ng? They were quite fixated on the story." He smiled at me, his lips parting only slightly, just enough for me to spy the tips of his incisors glowing unnaturally white.

I cleared my throat and glanced at Daniel. He was rolling the mouthpiece of his pipe along his tongue and staring hard at Jayce, but he said nothing. "I would guess it's a horror story, then?" I asked.

The designer opened his mouth to respond, but Daniel interrupted him. "Now, Jayce, that's not a very kind thing to say. I thought you were quite happy with the book proof." He rested his pipe next to the host's hip, then stretched his arms to rest them along the back of the tub, his left hand only inches from my shoulder. "A collector." He huffed in jest and reached forward to graze his fingertips along the top of my arm.

Jayce immediately stood up and leaned down, bringing his face only inches from Daniel's "You're a fucking vampire and we both know it," he whispered.

Daniel did not flinch. "And *you* still have to sign off on the galleys. Why don't you drop by the office Monday morning and we'll give them a look together, yeah?" His voice was even, his gaze frozen on the designer's, and I felt my stomach quiver uneasily, unsure of what was about to happen next.

After a long uncomfortable minute, Jayce stood tall again. He ran long fingers through his short brown hair and looked at me again. His green eyes narrowed like a cat's. "The nonbinary look is in now," he said coolly and nodded an approval at me. "Bloody gorgeous *and* smart. Now you'll just have to work on the money."

I smiled weakly. "I'll do my best," I said, and I felt Daniel squeeze my arm almost imperceptibly.

That Monday morning, I arrived early to work, having caught the earlier train from West Medford and forgoing my usual stop at the Starbuck's on the corner. Xanadu's offices were sprawled across the top floors of a converted brownstone a few blocks from the Common. The nearby hotel suite, I discovered after our initial meeting, was Daniel's permanent residence, the staff regularly tipped exorbitantly to be at his beck and call. He enjoyed walking to work and despised the subway, he explained to me. "There is no use being underground if you can avoid it," he said. "We're not fucking mole people."

"But if you start, for Christ's sake, use a condom," Lisa quipped from her desk in the office next door, not bothering to look up from her laptop screen. More often than not, Lisa worked from home, the commute from her Salem home unnecessary when most of her day was spent editing manuscripts alone. Daniel met exclusively with the big-name celebrity clients, leaving Lisa to deal with the handful of everyday people whose memoirs they'd published. "Accident porn," she clarified. "The rubber-neck stories of Daddy diddlers and adolescent alcoholics. As much as families avoid talking about these dumpster fires at the kitchen table, they dive head-first into the flame when it's bound in hardcover."

"Schadenfreude?" I offered. I could count on one hand the number of times Lisa had acknowledged me and savored any attention she deemed me worthy.

"Plain, old-fashioned creep curiosity, more likely," she answered. Then, she shut the door to her office. I hadn't seen her since, her only proof of life the occasional curt email replying to my assessments of slush pile manuscripts.

It wasn't unusual, then, for Xanadu's offices to be dark and silent when I keyed into the main entrance just after seven A.M.. It *was* unusual, however, to smell the familiar sweet pungency of Daniel's pipe tobacco so early in the day, but before I felt along the wall to turn on the overhead lights, I could see a faint fog of smoke suspended in front of the windows, the tall panes naked save for a few corners delicately edged with late autumn frost. I paused and listened. Above me to the left, I heard the muffled voices. Men. The timbre of the conversation was even, friendly, but I could not make out the words.

I shrugged off my winter coat and hung it on the rack, then tapped the tips of my shoes on the carpet to shake off any residual snow that had stuck to their soles. My office was the small one just off the foyer, but I leaned inside only to drop my shoulder bag on a nearby chair. Curious, I walked quietly to the other end of the hall and climbed the open stairway to the next floor.

The top floor of the brownstone had been renovated so that three of the smaller rooms, those on the front side of the building, comprised one large office, Daniel's office, complete with a kitchenette and full bathroom. The remainder of the floor housed Luke's office, though I had yet to see the promotion chief since submitting my employment paperwork. Most meetings, I learned, were conducted behind closed doors, and often outside of banker's hours. Daniel's door was not completely closed; it hung slightly ajar as if beckoning me closer, a stream of light illuminating an inch-wide bar on the hall carpet. The muffling voices had quieted, but I could still hear someone rustling about within, so I tip-toed toward the door and cautiously peered inside.

To the right, Daniel's pipe lay abandoned in a silvery isinglass ashtray on his dark wood desk, a thin trail of smoke still whispering from it into the air. To the left, Daniel stood hunched over the room's oversized sofa, its wide berth artfully arranged kitty-corner with one arm touching the exposed brick wall and the other pointing toward the southeast-facing windows, three of which jutted outward in a hexagon shape so that the right end of the couch nestled cozily within its nook, bathing the seating area with natural light nearly all-day long. It was at this end that Daniel stood, his broad frame blocking out the bright winter sun and coloring his shape in partial shadow. I could see that his back was turned to me and he was folding a large bundle of deep green fabric that lay in an awkward clump on the cushions.

I rapped softly on the door. "Daniel, I—"

He spun around to look at me, taken by surprise, and the bundle on the couch stirred. It wasn't a bundle at all, but Jayce, lying on his back and swathed in an emerald-colored pashmina, his legs starkly naked but folded up toward his stomach in an awkward yoga pose.

I squinted, willing my eyes to adjust to the bright light. "Daniel, I'm sorry. I came in early. I hope you don't mind," I said, my voice trailing off like someone had turned the volume knob in my mouth down abruptly. I stared as the image in front of me emerged into focus, my body frozen.

Daniel's mouth was agape, his toothless gums

visibly wet. His pupils had swallowed any brightness in his eyes; the now familiar black marbles shone expressionless at me. My employer pressed his lips together like a girl fixing a fresh layer of lip gloss, blinked his eyes, and cleared his throat. "You've come just in time," he said. His voice was scratchy, gurgling, full of acid. "Jayce was just signing off on the final proof." He waved his hand sideways, pointing vaguely in the direction of his desk. "Have a seat. It's time you learned this step of the process." As he finished saying this, the wet membranes of his gums pressed together, then ripped apart, creating an audibly moist smack.

I hesitated, then edged slowly sideways, keeping my eyes on my monstrous employer and the beautiful reality star paused in this surreal tableau, until my thigh nudged the front of Daniel's desk. Jayce's eyes were open, glazed and unmoving, but I could see a rhythmic swelling and contracting in his chest. I quickly grabbed one of the visitor's chairs and turned it to face the couch and sat down. "What is this?" I asked. "What are you doing?" When Daniel did not respond right away, I added, "Is he okay?"

"He's just fine," black-eyed Daniel answered wetly.

Without further elaboration, he turned back to his project, this time, angling his body so that I could view him from the side and his chest faced Jayce's torso. As if resuming an everyday task, Daniel methodically opened his mouth wide, violently snatched Jayce's legs by the calves, and pulled the designer's bare feet to his lips. It was then that Daniel's mouth seemed to double, then triple in size, the lower half of his face swelling like a balloon, his bare gums stretching painfully apart to form a red, aqueous chasm. Before I could blink, Jayce's feet disappeared within its depths and Daniel's lips wrapped themselves snugly around the lovely upper calves, forming a tight seal. I watched the round lump of his throat bob twice, three times, and heard the deep gurgling as the designer's appendages snaked their way down his esophagus and into his stomach.

Daniel pulled away and stood up straight again, and Jayce's legs, what remained of them, dropped like discarded stones onto the sofa, bouncing slightly. They had been severed just below the knee, a smooth covering of soft, new skin already capping the ends like new pencil erasers. The limbs had been cauterized. I glanced again at Jayce's face. His eyes remained in a trance and his expression belied nothing of what had just transpired.

I looked again at Daniel. He was holding his jaw, readjusting the dentures he'd replaced in his mouth. "I don't understand," I said.

Daniel removed his hand from his chin and placed it on his head, checking for any hair out of place. "What is confusing to you?" he asked. His eyes and appearance had returned to normal; the only clue that something nefarious had transpired was the hobbled client beside him.

I pointed to Jayce. "You…you ate him," I said, then laughed at the absurdity of the statement.

Daniel walked to the other end of the couch and reached beside it, retrieving his discarded suit jacket and putting it on. "I consumed him," he corrected. "His feet, anyway." He ran his hands along the jacket's lapel and smoothed an imaginary wrinkle. "Years of three inch heels always take their toll in the end. He wasn't too crazy about the galleys, either, but I think I've taken care of both. Two birds." He walked toward me, then turned sharply and walked behind his desk, finally settling into its high-backed leather chair. "Goddamn celebrities. Always forgetting shite. Lesson number two: keep most of the negotiation in writing: texts and email. They're so used to being catered to, all of their professional careers. It cultivates this…I suppose it's a form of misappropriated OCD. And the drugs, or the booze, or maybe just too much goddamn pussy…" He winked at me when he said this, but I stared back at him blankly. "Whatever it is," he continued unfettered, "it makes them forget what they insisted was so goddamn important just a week previous."

"And you amputate their legs to jog their memory?" I asked, deadpan. There was something comical about the whole business, but darkly comical. I felt it bubbling just below the surface of our conversation. Gallows humor.

Daniel sighed. "*Symbiotic relationship,* my ingénue. Now you're the one with the short-term memory."

I looked at Jayce. The designer's eyes had closed. I couldn't remember if I'd seen Daniel do this or if Jayce had moved on his own. "Is he okay?" I repeated.

Daniel reached over and wrapped his hand around the stem of his pipe, pausing for a long moment before bringing the instrument to his mouth. "There are blankets in the cabinet on the wall." He jutted his head toward the exposed brick. "If you want to do something helpful, cover his legs up, keep him warm. He'll be staying here, on the couch, for about a week. Most of the time, he'll be unconscious, but in a stretch of brass monkey cold like we've been having, it's best we take precautions."

I did as Daniel advised, feeling my stomach lurch as I tucked the edges of the wool afghan under Jayce's naked stumps. "Now it's a casting couch," Daniel said, lighting his pipe.

I frowned. "I'm sorry?"

"You covered him in a throw," Daniel said, his mouth unsmiling. "Cast, throw. Get it?" He looked over at his computer screen and exhaled a stream of white smoke.

"At least he's in the sun," I said, looking out of the alcove toward the Commonwealth Avenue Mall, the tops of barren elm trees seeming to tickle the sky as they swayed in the frigid breeze. A small grey and white bird with markings like a black cap and eye mask landed on the sill and flittered for a moment, turned its head as if to peek inside, then took flight again. It knew when it was smarter to forgo the show, I remember thinking.

I, for my part, was not so smart.

I carefully leaned my wet umbrella against the wall near the firm's entrance, shivering in the coolness of the office air. I'd recently switched to taking the orange line to the Back Bay T-stop, as there were two coffee shops and a dry cleaners with an eight-hour turnaround on the short walk downhill from the subway station to Xanadu, but the downdraught of the wind between the John Hancock and opposite buildings captured and redirected the spring rainstorm sideways, pelting my body like a garden hose. My trench coat warded off most of the water, but from my knees down, I was soaked to the bone.

"Took the Clarendon Street corridor, did you?"

Luke's voice startled me, and I flinched, knocking

the top of the umbrella and toppling it to the Berber carpet floor. "Yes, the wind is pretty wicked there, isn't it?" I said, slightly embarrassed by my wet clothes.

The promotion chief stared at me from the bottom of the stairway. "It's actually quite refreshing in the summer humidity: you'll see," he said finally, his eyes traveling to my shins. "You'll want to dry those right away," he added, cocking an eyebrow. "Cheryl is on her way in to meet with Daniel, and he's going to need you to take notes for his email summary of their discussion."

I placed my coat on the rack and ran a hand through my hair, a bit damp from the horizontal spray. "How soon?" I asked, already feeling a bit sick from the chill.

Luke turned his wrist and glanced at his watch. "In the next hour or so. He's already upstairs. I'm sure I have an iron in my office." He assessed my wardrobe, smirking slightly. "Heat it up and run it along your pants legs. They look to be…cotton, right? Shouldn't harm the fabric as long as you don't go crazy with the setting."

I frowned. "You mean, steam them?" I tried

to imagine running a hot iron along my leg, the winter-ravaged skin on my calves crackling as it burned.

Luke placed a foot on the bottom step and his hand on the bannister. "Jesus, no. Come on. Follow me."

The promotion chief's office was larger than mine, larger than Lisa's, but seemed dim and cramped compared to Daniel's expansive, naturally lit workroom. Luke shut the door behind me and opened a sliding door to a deep closet, retrieving a silver iron. "I'll plug it in. You can use the couch. It's pretty firm." As he leaned down to reach the outlet, he looked back at me. "What are you waiting for? Take them off." He nodded at my pants.

When he looked away, I reluctantly unbuckled my belt and pushed my pants to the floor. The warm stagnant air tickled my bare legs, and I quickly stepped backwards and picked up the trousers to hold them in before me as a modesty shield. Without glancing my way, Luke left the warming iron on the nearby sofa and walked casually behind his desk. Bending over the couch seemed the most embarrassing position I could attain, so I sat neatly beside the pants and gingerly ran the iron back and forth along the wet fabric.

After a long silence, Luke looked up from his laptop screen. "It's good that I saw you," he said. "It's almost time for your nine-month review."

"Nine-month review?" I echoed, keeping my eyes fixed on my work.

"Right." Luke exhaled loudly and began to riffle through the top drawer of his desk, finally removing the iPad he'd held in front of me at the Book Fair the previous year. He rose from his chair and began to walk toward me.

"Wait," I said, hastily placing the iron on the ground and pulling the pants toward me, intent on putting them back on despite the slight dampness that remained.

Luke waved the air with his free hand. "It's just a head and shoulder shot. You're not a runway model."

Still, I lay the trousers across my bare thighs as I leaned back on the couch, forcing my shoulders back and my chin up. A quick shudder click sounded from the tablet and Luke walked back to his desk. I waited patiently for him to continue. When he didn't, I asked, "Is there a form I need to complete?"

Luke swiped his finger across the iPad screen, then looked up. "No, no. That's all there is to it."

I laughed nervously. "That's all? Just a photograph? That's my review?"

"It's a pretty accurate indicator of your progress," Luke said flatly. "Daniel is looking for growth."

I ran my hand along the bottom of the pants, then stood up to get dressed. "I think these are fine," I said. "They feel a little wet, but they look dry. Thanks for the help." I refastened my belt and smoothed my shirt. "I'll go check with Daniel."

"Stop back here after," Luke said, his eyes re-glued to his laptop screen. The iPad, its screen dark, remained on his desk. "There's something I want to show you."

"Will do," I answered, then unplugged the iron before leaving his office, closing the door behind me.

Cheryl Manning was approaching the top of the stairs as I walked by. "Good morning," I said brightly.

The music recording mogul grunted softly in my

direction, then turned toward Daniel's office. She pushed his door open without bothering to knock. "This city is a cesspool," she announced dramatically, and I filed in behind her. She walked immediately to the long couch beneath the wall of windows, sat down heavily, and began to fish through her large black handbag. "I can still smell the goddamn taxi on my clothes." She removed a burgundy leather case and selected a long white cigarette from its depths.

"I could have sent you a car," Daniel said, gliding over to her from his desk chair. He sat next to her on the sofa and produced a silver lighter, and the client leaned forward, placing the cigarette in her mouth and inhaling the flame until the tip glowed orange. "The Four Seasons didn't offer you one?" he continued, closing the top of the lighter and returning it to his jacket pocket.

Cheryl exhaled a stream of fetid gray smoke. "I'm at the Mandarin this time," she said. "Goddamn Boston. One way streets arranged every which way. It took the driver ten minutes to go five blocks." She wrapped her lips around the white filter again and sucked in deeply. "And this weather…nothing like

Los Angeles." Another plume of smoke.

Daniel smiled patronizingly and folded his hands together on his lap. "Yes, there are no earthquakes. And of course, unlike in Hollywood, here, I'm the only one of my kind. It keeps me in demand."

I sat down in Daniel's abandoned desk chair and snatched a yellow legal pad from atop his blotter, feeling around the space for an available pen.

Cheryl took another long drag, then reached behind her, pushing the bottom pane of the window open. As she blew the last traces of smoke from her lungs, she dropped the lit cigarette outside and closed the window again. Despite the continuing rain, I wondered if any passers-by had been the unlucky recipients of her unpleasant incendiary rap on their heads.

"So the cover," Cheryl said, crossing one black leathered leg over the other. "I think it should be a close-up of my face, just three-quarters showing." She held her hands in front of her head, the index fingers and thumbs sticking out like the corners of a picture frame. "Serious, you know? Intense."

Daniel pretended to consider her suggestion. "What made you think of this?" he asked. "Luke has a few mock-ups for you to—"

"Luke is a cunt," Cheryl said dismissively. "I don't like anything he's sent. They're all too weak, or trashy." She stood up and walked toward the bookshelf nestled within the exposed brick side wall. After scanning the spines, she pulled out a glossy paperback. "This. This is what I'm looking for." She held the book so that the cover faced Daniel. I knew which one she was holding, a ghostwritten biography of former professional wrestler that Xanadu had released a decade earlier. "Do you see this cover? This says powerful. It says *look at me*. That is what *my* memoir should say."

I jotted a few notes on the pad. *Three-quarters face shot. Power. Look at her.* I paused, added *Cunt*, but immediately scratched it out.

Daniel stretched his arms wide, resting them on the back of the sofa. "It says *In your face*. Is that how you want people to remember you? The woman who built a platinum record business from the ground up, all on her own? A one-woman trailblazer of rock and metal music for nearly two decades?" He raised his eyebrows and looked up at her in a mock pleading manner. "The manuscript isn't even finalized yet. Why don't we take a look at the draft next month and try to wring the essence from it then."

I made more notes on the yellow paper. *Trailblazer. Meeting next month. Wring the essence.*

Cheryl tossed the book onto a nearby end table as if returning it to the shelf were too arduous of a journey. "I thought you said it wouldn't be ready until the end of summer." She plopped back onto the couch like a pouting teenager.

Daniel placed his hand on her shoulder. "I'm thinking of having a fresh set of eyes take a gander at it. Light a fire under it. What are your thoughts on that?"

Cheryl paused. "A fluffer, you mean?"

"In a manner of speaking, yes," said Daniel. "Someone who will take the reins, give it the full-speed-ahead attention it deserves. I have just the eyes." He jutted his chin toward me. "My newest associate is fresh out of school. From your neck of the woods out West, if memory serves, yes?"

"Well, more northern—" I began.

"Oh," Cheryl interrupted, frowning in my direction. "I hardly noticed you were there." She looked at Daniel with a slight raise of her eyebrow. "One of these days, you'll hire some help that doesn't blend into the damn woodwork."

Daniel smiled widely. "Well, Cheryl, you know I've always been a fan of muted neutrals. They go with everything." He took her hand gently in his and brought it to his mouth in a delicate kiss. Instead of letting go immediately, he closed his eyes and breathed in deeply the scent of her skin, the edges of his grin still pricking the sides of his cheeks.

I looked down at the pad again, knowing what was likely to occur next. It was then that I saw the small wet circle on the yellow paper, a growing dark halo the size of a quarter. I touched it quizzically, then placed my hand on my mouth. Without my realizing it, a sliver of drool had leaked out from between my lips. I wiped the spot frantically with the tip of my finger.

"Not now." She pulled her arm back and shooed Daniel away with a wave of her hand. "I have an interview today with that dreadful tabloid." She slipped her phone from her purse and tapped the screen gently. "I do need a touch up, though. We can work something in this Friday, yes? You can come by the suite and buy me dinner first."

Daniel's smile remained frozen in place but the soft grumble from his stomach was audible even from my side of the room. "Of course. Friday it is," he said finally. "I'll come by at seven." He rested his hand between the buttons of his shirt, stood up, and stretched his other arm toward the door. "Shall we, then?"

Cheryl did not offer even a glance in my direction as Daniel escorted her downstairs, and I blended into the surroundings once more. As I was closing the door to Daniel's office, Luke appeared wordlessly in the threshold of his. He held out the iPad to me.

"I didn't forget," I said, though buoyed by the prospect of taking over the management of a book for such a big-name client, I had. I took the tablet from him and clicked the Home button to unlock it.

Luke breezed past me and toward the top of the

stairs. "Leave it on my desk when you're done," he said, then walked casually down and out of immediate sight.

I held up the screen, tilting it slightly to garner a better view. As I swiped back and forth, the image of me vacillated from the one at the Book Fair and the one of me less than an hour before. I opened Daniel's office again and walked directly to the windows, hoping the brighter light would offer some explanation, but none came. The headshots were framed exactly the same way and had been taken from the same angle, and yet, there was a marked difference between them.

My jaw, or rather, the area from my cheekbones to my neck, had changed. The transformation was barely noticeable without a side-by-side comparison, but indeed, my mouth was slightly swollen.

On one of those strange New England Saturdays with weather that straddled the seasons of spring and summer, I struggled trying to open the windows connecting the living room with the three-season porch. The ancient paint had settled and cemented the heavy, ancient sashes in place. After a great deal of effort, I was finally able to free one of the windows and push one of the frames upward, the rush of warm, green air a welcome addition to the stuffy first floor.

Exhausted and slightly irritated, I sat for a moment on the couch in my childhood home and focused, for the first time that day, on what was on the television screen. Often, I turned on the set when I was getting ready for work or cooking in the adjacent kitchen just to provide some background noise and keep me from disappearing into my thoughts. The channel where I had last tuned happened to be one now featuring a daytime talk show, one of those celebrity-gossip cooking-demo hybrids where the lighting and camera filters made everyone's skin look slightly smudged.

I edged forward on the cushion when I saw the episode's featured guest. Jayce, a chiseled statue of masculine beauty, sat breezily in one of those metal bar stools on which anyone else would have looked slightly uncomfortable, his toned silhouette clothed in an expensive-looking suit jacket and trousers. As he crossed one leg over another, I caught a glimpse of the antiqued leather oxfords on his feet. My doorbell rang, and I reached over to press MUTE on the remote control that sat on the end table.

To my surprise, I found Daniel standing on the other side of the screen door. Despite the growing heat, he was wearing the same suit he'd worn when we first met at the Book Fair. I glanced behind him, unsure of how he might have traveled. I didn't think he owned a car. "Daniel," I said. "Hello."

"How are you?" he answered, his eyes darting about my porch.

"I…" I rested my hand on the door handle but did not turn it. "Is something wrong?" Daniel had never come to my house, never had a reason to even know where I lived, and I'd never volunteered the information except on the employment paperwork I returned to Luke. Had he gone through my file to find me, and if so, why do so when he could have called?

His eyes finally landed back on mine. "I was in the neighborhood, and I thought I'd drop in," he said. He flashed his cartoon cat grin, and I half expected his eyes to darken and glaze; I gripped the handle tighter in automated response. When I made no further move, he added, "May I come in?"

I opened the door and reluctantly ushered my employer inside, only then realizing that I was dressed in a pair of old sweatpants and a t-shirt stained by a long ago painting endeavor. "I'm sorry. If I had known you'd be coming by, I would have been more presentable." I waved to my left, toward the living room sofa. "Please, come and sit down."

Daniel walked slowly into my house, placing each foot solidly on the hardwood floor of the entranceway, then on the soft blue shag. As he padded toward the seating area, I closed the door. "How did the meeting go last night?" I asked. Daniel had flown to Los Angeles that Wednesday to meet with a producer about a movie documentary adaptation of one of Xanadu's celebrity memoirs. He looked a bit tired, and I realized too late that this likely meant the negotiation had not gone as planned. I bit my lip in penance for my misstep and began again. "I'm sure that—"

"I'm so sorry. I didn't realize you had company."

I hadn't seen Mom—outside of awkwardly brief Zoom calls between two floors—since the previous summer, and I hadn't heard her soft steps down the center stairway. Her voice sounded oddly melodic after hearing it exclusively over technology for the past year.

"I heard the doorbell and thought it might be a delivery. I didn't know you were home," she continued. Her hair had grown out awkwardly, I noticed, the ash brown pixie now a jumbled fright sticking aloft and snaking apprehensively around the sides of her neck. Her skin, once smooth and taut, was grey and puffy.

Daniel, however, seemed completely unfazed by her appearance and walked immediately toward my mother with his arm outstretched. "I'm Daniel."

She shook his hand softly then ran her fingers self-consciously over her hair. "Ah, you're the publisher employing my lovely housemate," she said.

"I am," said Daniel. He rested his hand on his chest and jauntily tucked his fingers between the buttons on his shirt. "I'm fortunate to have found quite a protégé."

I shifted from one foot to the other, feeling like the child interloper at a parent-teacher conference. Daniel was staring at my mother in such a focused manner, I felt my discomfort grow even more pressing. "Can I get you anything, Mom?" I asked.

"What?" Mom looked distracted, as if I'd interrupted a complicated thought. "No, no, nothing. I'm sorry to have intruded." She turned to look at Daniel. "I've become a bit of a ghost in my own house, I'm afraid," she said. "Well then, I'm off to continue peeling yellow wallpaper off the attic walls." Before either of us could respond, she scurried back up the stairs, her stocking feet making hushed whispers on the hardwood treads.

"Seems a bit out of sorts, that one," Daniel said, his eyes traveling up the banister, appearing to follow my mother back to her third-floor hideaway.

"My father passed away suddenly," I explained, suddenly feeling protective. "They were together for thirty years, traveled all over the place."

He thought for a moment, moving his hand from his shirt to his pants pocket. "Perhaps she's in need of a little rejuvenation."

"She's not a client, and she's not in need of anything," I said quickly, my voice firm, "so you can take that dinner off the table." The clipped manner of my statement took even me by surprise.

Daniel walked back to the sofa and sat down, emitting a small groan of relief as his body sank into the fabric. He looked down at his feet. "This is some carpet," he remarked, and reached his hand down to run his fingers through the long blue fibers.

I rested a hand on my hip. "I don't mean to be rude, Daniel, but—"

"But you are." My employer's voice dropped two octaves and flattened.

I paused and slowly took in a breath. "I apologize, but I was just about the start cleaning the—"

Daniel nodded at the television, its screen still showing the silent movie of Jayce nodding and smiling politely as the vapid talk show host yammered on excitedly. "Looks as though you were catching up on your daytime media garbage." He glanced around the side table. "Can you turn it up a bit? I'm curious to hear what he has to say about his pending release."

At that moment, however, the show dissolved into a commercial break, a popular female comedian accosting women in bathrooms with tampons. I walked to the side table and patiently clicked the

OFF button on the remote. "I really didn't mean to be, Daniel. What can I do for you?" I sat down next to him, recalling almost immediately how the seating arrangement mirrored our first meeting together in his hotel suite.

Daniel leaned backwards and rested his hand again inside his button placket again. Even in a strange place, in an unfamiliar suburb, my employer always looked at home. "It's time you learned the rest of the business. I promised to train and nurture you in this profession, and it's been nearly a year." He raised an eyebrow. "I take it you've seen a great many exceptional and curious things in your work with me."

My back stiffened. "I have," I began slowly. "You showed me more than I could have ever imagined. But…" I looked down at my knees.

Daniel reached over and placed his large hand on the leg closest to him, and I flinched. "Tell me, then. Why won't you let me near your mother?"

I looked him in the eye. "My mother?"

Daniel removed his hand and gestured toward the

stairway. "Just now. Your mother believes she is fading away: she admitted it to you, just now." He replaced his hand, patting my lower thigh like one might do a loyal pet. "You have seen what happens. She will be as good as new when I am done. Better than new." He continued his rhythmic patting.

"I thought you fed on knowledge within the profession, practical experience, celebrity," I argued. "She's never worked in the industry."

Daniel grinned, a Cheshire cat's devious sneer. "I said I feed on experience. I never said publishing experience." He squeezed my knee and lifted his hand, punctuating this statement with a wave of his fingers. "Why do you think I specialize in memoir? They're trite, masturbatory garbage. The celebrities… all they care about is staying relevant, being seen. If they aren't being watched by strangers, they don't exist. Holograms: that's what they are, really. They have no 'skin in the game,' you might say."

I backed away slightly. "I don't understand what you're saying."

Daniel smiled again, patronizing me. "You wanted

to know the publishing business. This is it, my ingénue. Memoirs are only one course of the meal; a tapas buffet, if you will. Select substantial ones and they can feed you morning, noon, and night, and without much of the fuss of figuring out what genre the market is hot for that year. People are voyeurs at heart. There will always be readers interested in peeking over a stranger's fence and getting an eyeful. And the juicier, the more horrific the life story, the tastier.

"However, all writing, all writers who wish to be published, it, they are the same at the core. All of them want to be read, remembered, *cherished*." He sighed and rested his hand on his own knee. "Human bodies wear down," he continued. "They give out. No one is immortal, not without help. All writers wish to live forever, don't they? Even if they won't admit it. They vomit up these sacred parts of themselves, wrap those shards in paper, and pray the remnants will exist long after they are decomposing in the grave. Publishers grant them that wish. We take what they offer, and we digest it, repackage it, shine it showroom new, and suddenly, it's those bits, those pieces *we've* taken in, that are no longer decaying. And we'll exist long after that writer is gone, to profit from their bodily humors."

I folded my arms across my chest. "Jayce was right. You are a collector. A vampire."

Daniel stood up and stretched languidly, stifling a yawn. "This is the profession you chose, my *graduate-degree-in-English*." He laughed: a bitter, sadistic chortle. "What in God's name did you expect to do with that, exactly? You paid for a concentrated study in reading and writing." He laughed again.

I stood up as well. "You eat people. It's not the same as publishing people's stories."

Daniel smiled sardonically. "Isn't it?"

We both stared at one another. After a long pause, Daniel reached his hand toward my face and gently ran his first two fingers along my cheekbone, as Jayce had once done. I moved my face away, and he gruffly grasped my chin in his hand, turned my face to meet his again, and held it there. Before I could think, I grabbed his wrist and wrenched his hand away, then changed my mind and pulled his fingers toward my mouth and bit down, hard.

Daniel did not flinch, but he did gently remove his hand from my mouth, holding it between us in the air as if to taunt me into performing the act again. "Naughty, but you've got the right idea. As I said, being a cannibal is the only way to truly succeed in this business." He wiped his hand on his pinstriped shirt and looked over at the staircase. "Now where did you say that mother disappeared to?"

He was still looking to his right when I pushed him, hard, in the center of his breastbone, then kicked at his knees as powerfully as I could. Daniel buckled, his mouth twisting in an expression of both surprise and what appeared to be a glimmer of admiration. As he toppled sideways, I sprang onto him, pushed his back flat against the thick carpet, and straddled his bulging torso. He began flailing his arms, slapping and scratching at my face, his fingers reaching desperately to snag themselves in my flesh. I shimmied my legs forward to pin his upper arms to the ground.

"What—" Daniel began, but I leaned sideways and shoved his right hand in my mouth again, this time, biting down as hard as I could muster, feeling the flesh give way between my teeth and the warm innards escape from the confinement of skin and ooze under my tongue. Daniel pulled his left arm from under my weight and sank his fingers into the small of my back, but I bit again and again, finally feeling the bones in the center of his right hand separate and my jaws tear the top half of his palm free.

As his arm flopped back down to his side, blood spirting from the severed appendage, my first instinct was to spit out the mouthful of fingers. However, my eyes caught sight of Daniel's expression. For the first time in the whole year that I had known him, he looked exhausted. Beaten. Weak.

I had a better idea.

I chewed, my tongue grazing the hard callouses of skin, my teeth masticating the flesh until it softened. My mouth dripped warm, salty blood and sinewy muscle as I fished sticks of bone from between my lips and held them up for both of us to curiously examine. They were ivory, almost tan in color, like fragments of a turkey wishbone, and I tossed the remnants onto the carpet of thick blue yarn next to us.

"Can't stomach all of it, can you?" Daniel taunted,

panting. Despite our tousling, his face was ghastly white, an expressionless corpse.

I rolled the last bit of carpal bones against the inside of my mouth, then swallowed hard, feeling the hard bolus work its way down my throat and into my chest. I smiled down at Daniel, feeling the residue of my act sticking to my teeth and gums. My employer stared hard at me for a moment, then folded forward in a half-hearted crunch, immediately falling backward again in an attempt to throw me from his body. I held tight to his shoulders as he bucked wildly, and for a long moment, we were the beast with two backs, one head snapping and growling and the other sweating in panic and exhaustion.

When I lifted myself backwards and met his eyes once more, I noticed his face beginning to change. The membranes just beneath his poreless skin flushed crimson with blood, his jaw stretched and elongated, and his eyes swelled up and darkened into dead, round marbles. He folded forward again, angling his hungry, gaping maw toward my face, and I flailed desperately in my attempt to escape it. I struck Daniel across the mouth, right along those widening lips, and sent his dislodged chiclet smile flying across the air, landing on the hardwood floor near the staircase where it skidded to a stop. Before I could lose my nerve, I bent down and clamped my own teeth on his lower lip and tore, ripping the flesh from his skull and forcing myself to swallow it.

Even when Daniel cried out in a desperate plea for reprieve, for mercy, I did not stop.

It was the squeak of the mail slot, announcing the arrival of a few skinny envelopes as they sailed onto the foyer floor, inches away from Daniel's discarded teeth, that brought me back to attention. Hours had passed. I felt nauseated and my head pounded. Nothing remained of my employer but a pool of residual blood and sinew and a damp, creature-shaped outline composed of couture clothing. I was kneeling in an inch of thick, red liquid, and everything smelled metallic, coppery, with the faintest hint of burnt vanilla.

I did my best to keep him down. I promised myself I wouldn't regurgitate Daniel. I concentrated instead on my breathing, on quelling the itchy revulsion swelling inside of me.

My cell phone trilled jubilantly from the kitchen where I had left it on the table that morning, Mom's ringtone. I considered what I will tell her. No, her delivery had not yet arrived. No, I still hadn't uncovered any of her jewelry lurking in the lush blue carpet…not yet, but I did find something else, something much, much more valuable.

I wiped my mouth. Luke's iPad images hadn't lied: it was definitely bigger. Elongated. Swollen. My teeth ached, and a few of them felt loose. I poked a finger at an incisor and it wiggled.

When I could finally stand, I patted my distended belly and breathed in slowly. I could feel the stench of Daniel's life essence oozing down my legs, swimming in my saliva, caking every inch of my skin. Everywhere I looked, I was red, my outsides drying solidly to a deep brick color.

I was bloody gorgeous. But Daniel was right.

It would never be enough.

Rebecca Rowland is the American dark fiction author of The Horrors Hiding in Plain Sight, Pieces, The View Master, and Optic Nerve and the curator of six horror anthologies, including the bestseller Unburied: A Collection of Queer Dark Fiction. Her short fiction, guest essays, and book reviews regularly appear in a variety of publications and horror websites. She is an Active member of Horror Writers Association, makes her home in a landlocked and often chilly corner of New England, and listens a little too closely to detailed stories of horrifying surgical procedures. Drop by to visit her at RowlandBooks.com: she won't make you take your shoes off, but a nice cheese plate is always appreciated.